This book belongs to:

_____

For Ray, whose spirit infuses these pages,
and for Jai, who listens to all my questions.

Huge thanks to English Heritage, the University of Cambridge Digital Library and
http://darwin-online.org.uk for making it possible for me to research this book, and thanks
to the wonderful staff at Down House for answering all my questions and creating and
maintaining such a wonderful place to visit. Any errors are entirely mine!

Copyright © 2021 by Lauren Soloy

Tundra Books, an imprint of Penguin Random House Canada Young Readers, a division of
Penguin Random House of Canada Limited

Library and Archives Canada Cataloguing in Publication

Title: Etty Darwin and the four pebble problem / Lauren Soloy.
Names: Soloy, Lauren, author, illustrator.
Identifiers: Canadiana (print) 20200215388 | Canadiana (ebook) 20200215396 | ISBN 9780735266087
   (hardcover) | ISBN 9780735266094 (EPUB)
Subjects: LCSH: Litchfield, Henrietta Emma Darwin, 1843-1929—Juvenile fiction.
Classification: LCC PS8637.O4472 E88 2021 | DDC jC813/.6—dc23

Published simultaneously in the United States of America by Tundra Books of Northern New York, an imprint of
Penguin Random House Canada Young Readers, a division of Penguin Random House of Canada Limited

Library of Congress Control Number: 2020936827

Edited by Samantha Swenson
Designed by Emma Dolan
The artwork in this book was rendered in watercolors, pencils, crayons, pastels,
gouache, papers, ink and pixels using brushes, scissors, glue sticks and love.
The text was set in Adobe Caslon Pro and Carrotflower

Printed and bound in China

www.penguinrandomhouse.ca

1 2 3 4 5   25 24 23 22 21

Penguin
Random House
TUNDRA BOOKS

tundra

ETTY DARWIN

- AND THE -
FOUR PEBBLE PROBLEM

Lauren Soloy

tundra

Once there was a girl named Henrietta Darwin.
She preferred to be called Etty, thank you very much.

Her father, Charles, was one of the greatest thinkers
in the history of the World.

He'd made himself an oval thinking path called The Sandwalk, so he could walk while he thought, which he did every day, twice a day.

Sometimes Etty joined him.

The Sandwalk

They would begin by deciding how many times to go around and then setting out flint pebbles to keep track.

Some days Etty would ask her Papa a question that she'd been pondering.

She didn't always like the
answers he gave her ...

I have trouble believing in
anything without proof.

Oh.

Sometimes I think I see a fairy. But then it turns out to be a bird. Or a leaf.

...But she did like how he never treated her questions as childish or silly.

Or perhaps sometimes we just need to look a little closer. Like these butterflies.

What butterflies?

Sometimes Etty thought
of new questions . . .

Do butterflies
live everywhere in
the world?

North America
Europe
Africa
South America
I've found butterflies every place I've ever been.
Except the middle of the ocean.

. . . That often led to more questions.

At times, on the ocean, there is nothing living, as far as the eye can see. It is very lonely.
But, Papa...

...What about all of the creatures under the water?
You're right, of course.

Sometimes Etty learned new information as they walked . . .

For example, see this flat patch of grass?
Yes?
That, combined with this hole, is evidence that a fox rested here, after a delicious meal of worms.

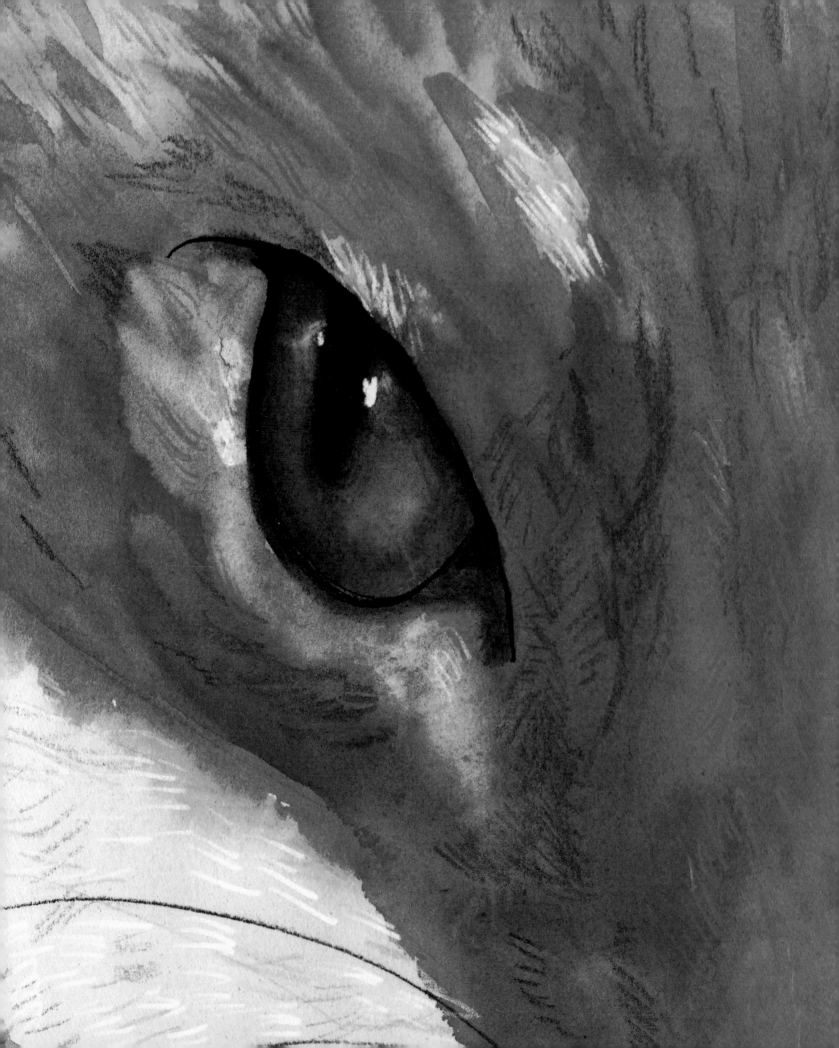

And sometimes that information led to new ideas.

Maybe we just don't know what to look for yet? To prove that fairies exist?

Could be.

and playing all day with the birds and the animals...
I want to BE a fairy!

...And sometimes Etty thought of answers.

Papa, I know I can't figure out how to prove
that fairies are real, but...

But, no matter the weather, or the reason, whether she got answers or just more questions ...

...Being under the trees and the sky
gave Etty's thoughts space to fly.

I feel better after
our walk, don't you?

Charles Darwin was one of the most important thinkers of the 1800s. He was interested in everything one could find in the natural world — from beetles to orchids to facial expressions. But what interested him most was *why* things are the way they are. After many adventures, including sailing around the world and studying animals no one had ever studied before, Charles settled at Down House with his wife, Emma, to work and write and enjoy their growing family.

The Darwins eventually had ten children, including Etty. When Etty grew up, she became an important helper in Charles Darwin's work, and he valued her opinion as a fellow thinker. She actually edited some of his writing! As a child, though, she used the backs of his original manuscripts as scrap paper, to draw pictures and write fairy stories. The Darwin house sounds like a fun house to grow up in — there was a slide on the stairs and a rope hanging down on the first floor landing to use as a swing!

Charles did most of his thinking on daily walks around the oval path he made for just this purpose: The Sandwalk. And his children were always welcome to walk with him. Down House is a museum today, and you can still wander along the same path that the Darwins did. However, you can also create your own thinking path, wherever you happen to be. Walking is a wonderful way to contemplate big questions. You don't have to know the answers — sometimes it's enough to think of the questions!

Everything in my story is based on actual people and events. While I can't be certain what Charles and Etty talked about on their walks, I like to think that fairies might have come up.